I0640704

Alfred Robinson

California

An historical poem

Alfred Robinson

California
An historical poem

ISBN/EAN: 9783743463554

Manufactured in Europe, USA, Canada, Australia, Japa

Cover: Foto ©Andreas Hilbeck / pixelio.de

Manufactured and distributed by brebook publishing software (www.brebook.com)

Alfred Robinson

California

CALIFORNIA:

AN HISTORICAL POEM.

BY

ALFRED ROBINSON,

Author of "Life in California."

SAN FRANCISCO:
WILLIAM DOXEY.
1889.

To

THE PIONEERS OF CALIFORNIA

THIS WORK

IS RESPECTFULLY DEDICATED BY

THE AUTHOR.

PREFACE.

The following Poem is an attempt to delin-
eate and expose the eccentricities of a country
whose sudden rise and progress have no par-
allel in the world's history; and, in the many
allusions to them, the author would remark
that none are intended as personal, but, on
the contrary, mere outlines of events, transpir-
ing during the first period of California, under
a new and alien system of government.

SAN FRANCISCO, 1889.

INTRODUCTION.

When Roman zeal had forced its way and gained
A footing on the western shore, and when
Brave souls to raise the cross and spread their faith
Within a savage land had risked their lives—
'T was then a place was sought their patron saint
To dedicate. A spacious bay inclosed
By fertile lands, whose hills and vales were stored
With wondrous wealth, through which bright
    rivers roll'd
And spread their golden sands o'er all the plains
Around. The woods and glens were rife with
    game,
And there the wily Indian roamed, to chase
The deer, or there the grizzly bear to hunt
And fearless slay. Oft to some rude steep he
Climb'd, and ling'ring on the lofty height, hailed
There with joy the scene that lay beneath. But

Ah! a frown his swarthy brow did cross, when
On a gentle mound his piercing eye did
Rest, near which at work some zealous priests the
Pathless woods were felling, and where clusters
Of the savage tribes were busy too, a
Place to clear, that there they might a Christian
Temple build and elevate the cross.   For
Rapid strides the Fathers made, and daily
To their righteous fold did many converts
Gain.   Along the hills and neighb'ring shores
    were
Other stations, and at every one, they
Prospered well; whilst here and there, the
    gardens
Green and cultured fields that might be seen,
    gave
Ample proof of how the Fathers lived.   The
Warrior too, gave sterling aid, and arm'd
With buckler, pike and blade, protection gave,
As briskly on, the conquest went, for Priest
And Soldier, both, would save the savage soul.

PREAMBLE I.

One eve, as I rambled, not far
     from the city,
A poor woman I happened
     to meet;
Who said to me sadly, "Good sir,
     pray have pity,
And quick give me relief I
     entreat.

" Since the morn's early dawn, in vain I've
sought food,
To keep my starved children from
crying,
A trifle from you sir, will do
the babes good,
And save them most surely from
dying."

" Then haste thee, good mother," I said,
" and be fleet,"
As I pressed in her hand a
gold coin ;
" With this ye can buy them abundance
to eat,
So away, thy young starvelings
to join."

Resuming my ramble, so sadly
    suspended,
She said, ''Stay, I have something
    for thee ;
For kindness like thine to those thus
    befriended,
A requital should have, sir,
    from me.

''Accept then this optic, its
    mystical sight,
Will the past like the present
    display,
And things that have perished will bring
    back to light,
Though to mem'ry long faded
    away.''

So homeward I hurried, o'erjoyed
at the thought
That now I could fathom my
neighbor ;
A test was soon made on a knave
whom I sought
Whose faults were exposed without
labor.

And bound now to visit the great
growing North,
Where the sages had built a large
village ;
I packed up my treasure with which
I set forth,
To discover their scheming and
pillage.

A few days at sea brings us close
    to the scene
  Where swift up the bay we are
    gliding ;
The current moves rapid, the wind
    it blows keen,
  And soon, we at anchor are
    riding.

Now, Ho ! for a peep at the great
    golden city,
  And I raise the charmed gift to
    my eye ;
But what do I see?   Oh, great God,
    in thy pity,
  Pray forgive all the faults I
    descry !

Aloft, e'en above the high
        telegraph peak,
Amid clouds of bright silver
        and gold ;
An eaglet doth soar, with this scroll
        ,   in her beak:
Here both *Justice* and *Conscience*
        are sold.

More central is seen the fair Goddess
        of Fame,
Her eyes glaring wild and
        in ire ;
A book lies before her—she points
        to its name,
'T is written in letters
        of fire—

SAN FRANCISCO.

CANTO I.

Two rapid streams from ages known,[1]
That in their course conjoined had grown,
    The legends tell;
And flowing on, o'er vast domains,
Through flowery meads and grassy plains,
    A lake did swell.

Whence bursting o'er its rocky bound,
Their ceaseless flow bold egress found,
    Thus fresh and fair;
To sportive join the briny deep,
Therein to rage, or there to sleep
    With waveless care.

And flowing on, still swift they ran,
E'er deep'ning where their breach began
　　Its shallow strait;
Till by their flow was oped a way,
Disclosing now a spacious bay,
　　In pristine state.

Where 't was that came in after years,[2]
That holy band of Pioneers,
　　Of whom we read;
Whose active zeal did thousands win
From Pagan rites and Pagan sin
　　To Rome's fair creed.

And once a year a gallant sail,
From Castile's shore, with Royal mail,
　　Then cheered the port;
Where safely moored, for months she lay,
Dispensing out, from day to day,
　　The aid she brought.

But not till Spain's proud sway was o'er,[3]
Did other ships these wilds explore,
 Or traffic here;
And then so rare that they appeared,
Whene'er óne came, 't was gladly cheered,
 E'en far and near.

When in a nook that sheltered lay,
Called "Yerba Buena," in its day,
 The anch'rage ground;
Were bartered off the wares she brought,
In change for product found in port,
 At posts around.

And thus it was, those early days,
Gave little else of note to praise,
 From year to year;
Unless, perchance, some new-raised cot,
Or rustic cross, on some lone spot,
 The way to cheer.

Yet many an inroad had been made,
Ere progress dared to lift the shade
    Where darkness lay;
And then the task a hero braved,
As step by step, he boldly paved
    The cultured way.

A gallant Swiss, whose love of fame,[4]
Bestowed "Helvetia's" classic name
    On those broad lands;
Where he, so long, had chieftain been,
And where e'en now, his home is seen,
    And sightly stands.

At length a war with neighb'ring foes,[5]
Brought with it all the ills and woes
    That cause dismay;
When changed the scene before so bright,
For all its charms of old took flight,
    And passed away.

But haply here the strife was short,
For ships of war besieged the fort,
    Within the bay;
When all its posts, on either side,
Submissive bowed, with humbled pride,
    To alien sway.

And so, the foe, now sovereign here,
His laws proclaimed, afar and near,
    Throughout the land;
O'er which waved free, from many a height,
The emblem of his country's right,
    Long there to stand.

From which events we justly date,
The magic rise of this our State,
    To rank and name;
That in this bold, progressive age,
Takes signal part on history's page,
    Indeed, of fame.

For as progression forced its way,
To lands yet rude, o'er which held sway,
 A supine race ;
Its active march to light revealed
A golden tract, till now concealed,
 Of wondrous space.

Which news soon spread afar and wide,
Till freely told on every side,
 In statements rare,
That as they went, so wild they grew,
Their glowing tales the eager drew,
 To grasp a share.

For thus allured with hope of gain,
Their thousands formed a living chain,
 O'er land and sea ;
Whose thoughts by day, and dreams by night,
Of " *El Dorado* " visions bright,
 Gave joy and glee.

For gold it was, they frantic sought,
And 't was for gold the seas they fought,
 And tempests scorned ;
God only knows the victims dead,
Whose forms bestrew the ocean bed,
 Perchance unmourned !

Yet many a ship in triumph brought
Her living cargo safe to port,
 For transit here,
And truly 't was a treat to see,
These Argonauts on shore, set free,
 So full of cheer.

Indeed, in fleets they crossed our Gate,
Each gallant bark replete with freight, ·
 Of product rare ;
More prized than gems of precious gold,
For freights they were of freemen bold,
 And matrons fair.

That soon the barren hills made gay,
With thousands there, at work or play,
From morn till night ;
Whose armed display and tents around,
Had semblance to some battle-ground,
Or fortress height.

Whence now embarked they went in bands,
To seek, betimes, the golden lands,
Yet far away ;
And 't was indeed a merry sight,
To see them off, with hopes so bright,
And hearts so gay.

The *Sharp*, howe'er, saw golden cheer,
In daily schemes of profit here,
For him to rule ;
And soon to work his wits he set,
That he might draw within his net,
Some pliant tool.

The *Merchant,* too, remained behind,
A shelter for his wares to find,
    And give them care ;
For merchandise that came to hand,
And lay exposed upon the strand,
    Had perished there !

The *Landlord,* too, thought best to stay,
And in his own peculiar way,
    Do service here ;
Preparing homes with special care,
For those who sought his humble fare,
    And promised cheer.

The *Lawyer,* though, bright visions saw,
In counsel fees, and suits at law,
    That promised pay ;
And so to anchor quickly came,
To reap his share of all such game,
    That came in play.

The Court House then on "*Portsmouth Square*,"
Was oft the scene of judgments rare,
      And quaint decrees ;
And who doth not recall the way
The merchant service had to pay,
      Its fines and fees ?

For scarce a ship that reached the port,
But brought some knave who soon was sought
      A claim to make ;
And then divide the plunder got,
With him, who was the wily sot,
      The suit to take.

That tiny, dingy, loathsome Court !
'T was there the steamships first were sought,
      As legal prey ;
And dearly did their agent bleed,
To pay the sums the Court decreed
      To give away.

The *Gamester*, too, from choice remained,
Whose moral scruples ne'er restrained,
    His love for play ;
Nor luring to some modern hell,
The simple youth, who ever fell,
    An easy prey.

For all such dens, now served with care,
Adorned with gaudy trappings rare,
    The weak allured ;
And he, who ventured there to look,
Was trolled along to take the hook,
    And then secured.

What glaring sights were seen around,
When, in each street, the idler found
    A place like this !
When games of chance, and music too,
So charmed the crowds that thither drew,
    They thought it bliss.

At night, as one the streets did pace,
He saw, what seemed in every place,
    Some magic spell;
Where there the charms of song and dance,
That so the joys of life enhance,
    Did freely dwell.

And other scenes were blithe and gay,
Where tipplers passed their time away,
    Like sots of old;
And sat and talked morn, noon and night,
Of startling deeds, and bloody fight,
    For lust of gold.

The *Parson*, too, resolved to stay,
But not fair maid to give away,
    Oh, no indeed!
For maidens then were scarce, I ween,
And, in the town, too rarely seen,
    Such aid to need.

He tarried here, in hope, forsooth,
To lure some stray'd and fallen youth,
    From sin to prayer ;
And carry back to other days
His thoughts of home and early ways,
    When bright and fair.

The *Doctor*, too, attractions saw,
And, like the trickster of the law,
    Beheld his prey ;
For soon the miner, sore displeased,
Came limping from the mines, diseased,
    With means to pay.

And thus, a harvest, rich indeed,
Came pouring in, whilst hearts did bleed
    For friends of old ;
For brothers, or some other kin,
Who victims fell, to worldly sin
    Of lust for gold.

The graveyard then, o'er North Beach hill,
Betrayed the march of many an ill,
From day to day;
Whose grassy mounds the numbers told,
Of those, alas! both young and old,
That pass'd away.

Thus *hoary Time*, his transit sped,
And though fond hearts too oft had bled
At scenes like these,
The State at large had much to cheer,
For Mammon cast his treasure here,
The world to please.

And though its millions passed away
To other shores, from day to day,
In virgin gold;
They did not drain these staunch domains,
So rich were all the hills and plains
With wealth untold.

The *Sages*, wild at these extremes,
Began reform in all their schemes,
        Without delay;
And soon proposed their acts to crown,
By special change from chartered town
        To city sway.

When they, who held the public weal,
Did from the public eye conceal
        Their knavish plans;
By sales of lands and contracts, too,
'Mong those ycleped the chosen few
        Of favored clans.

But this, howe'er, was nothing new,
For oft the town had done so, too,
        In early days;
Though then esteemed of minor spoil,
And did not friends and foes embroil
        In wrangling frays.

But where bold peculation laid,
Was in the sales by *Sheriff* made,
    Of public land ;
To pay a judgment gained in law
By *Peter Smith*, who quickly saw
    The game on hand.

In sorry truth, sin grew apace,
And sowed its seeds in every place,
    To feast thereon ;
The city seeming all fair game,
For every one of vicious fame
    To prey upon.

It was, indeed, a "*Botany Bay*"
Of convict rogues, skilled every way .
    In fearful crime ;
Whose hellish scenes of dreadful fire,
And murder, too, that did transpire,
    Gave test in time.

The people roused at length, to ire,[6]
Resolved these fiends should hence retire,
  By force of arms ;
And formed at once, a gallant band,
Each member sworn to rid the land
  Of all such harms.

And well they kept their oaths, forsooth,
For prompt the rogues in every booth
  Were made secure ;
When one bold stroke on "Portsmouth Square,"
A hanging matter, did declare
  Their vengeance sure.

But, truly, 't was a sight most sad,
To thus behold a crowd, half-mad
  Gloat o'er its foe ;
But who can say the course pursued
Had not at least its moral good,
  Though crowned with woe !

A few such chast'nings spread alarm,
For soon the culprits fled from harm
    By land and sea ;
And through the State, the issue proved
A sovereign check, where treason moved,
    That left it free.

And now, triumphant over crime,
These guardsmen brave have left to time
    To solve their acts ;
And, in disbanding, each has placed
The part he took, to be retraced,
    And judged from facts.

PREAMBLE II.

A boat was now waiting, to take
    us on shore,
  With our luggage already
    therein ;
So quickly we followed, the town
    to explore,
  And in haste the grand work
    to begin.

On landing we rode to the nearest
    hotel,
O'er a sadly conditioned,
    rude pier ;
Whose planking was such though we passed
    o'er it well,
As to cause us, with reason,
    much fear.

For every few paces a hole
    was passed by,
Yawning wide to the waters
    below,
Where many a victim had drawn
    his last sigh,
As o'er him the current
    did flow.

The avenues, too, were quite out
    of repair,
So that jolting, we went all
    the way ;
Till reaching our lodgings, we paid
    the coach fare,
And alighted without more
    delay.

The famous " *Tehama* "! Yes, this
    was the place,
Whose lessee, Master Frink, at
    the door,
A welcome there gave us, with smiling
    good grace,
And a room on the second
    flight floor.

This *earthquake proof* mansion as oft
it was named,
Had escaped all the ravage
of fire,
Whose model was such as to make
it most famed
Of all others, when one did
retire.

Its windows were low, and a fine
balustrade
Encircled the building
around ;
From whence one with ease, o'er a light
palisade,
Could escape by a leap to
the ground.

But the time has gone by for this
kind of fear
No longer such dangers
alarm ;
The fireman is prompt, and treats
with a jeer
Every risk, so he saves us
from harm.

In fact, this Department, effective
and true,
Was made up from the bloods of
the town ;
Who for boldness of tact, and clev-
erness, too,
Have maintained far and near a
renown.

With this just admission, we pensive
lay down,
To reflect on the whims of
the day ;
And wondered if strangers that visit
the town,
Have observed, as we have, its
decay.

Its growth was too rapid, it merged
in a day,
As it spread o'er the hillocks
around,
And so will it vanish as quickly
away,
Until naught shall be left but
a mound.

Which fate the rude Indian doth sadly
    foreshow,
  When relating his legend
    of old ;
How a city would rise from regions ·
    below,
  And a sacrifice fall to
    its gold.

Five times has it happened, the omen
    't is plain,
  When destruction by fire
    ensued ;
But, Phœnix-like, rising to power
    again,
  The calamity may be
    renewed.

Come when it will come, there is hope
    for it left,
And a chance the sad presage
    to foil ;
Though deep are the wounds which disaster
    has cleft,
Yet it still may long prosper
    by toil.

Then courage, Franciscans ! On ye
    it depends,
Let misfortune come oft as
    it will ;
Be honesty thine, howsoe'er
    the tide wends
So that thus ye may yet
    triumph still.

The night passing o'er, we made haste
    now to test
The effect of our glass from
    the street ;
And took for our station, the point
    judged the best,
Where " *Montgom'ry* " with " *Jackson* "
    doth meet.

CANTO II.

Behold the *Past!*   There where you stand
The water rose at God's command,
  And bathed the shore.
Whence gentle springs, and streamlets fair
From out the gathered sand dunes there,
  Did freely pour.

And on your right, where yet is seen
The drama's once grand palace queen,
  A lakelet stood,
In which the wild-fowl oft did play,
When blustering winds swept o'er the bay,
  In angry mood.

And where *Commercial* cuts your street [7]
A mansion stood of frame complete
    And model fit ;
Whose halls oft rang with music's strain,
In love-told song, or sweet refrain,
    With frequent wit.

Its mistress then, a charming dame
Had far and near, reputed fame
    For grace and pride ;
Who, queen-like, at the festive board,
Oft joined her friends and true liege lord,
    To there preside.

It was the primal fabric then,
To cheer this lonely sea-side glen,
    So famed of yore ;
And mem'ry dear must first decay,
E'er charms so prized shall pass away,
    To charm no more.

And further on, a square, we 'll say,[8]
Where *California* spans the way
      Was Leidesdorff's pride ;
A tiny cottage, plain and neat,
And fairest gem that one could meet
      Then, far and wide.

With garden-plot of flowers rare,
Kept ever bright and ever fair
      By clever skill ;
From whence, abruptly, shooting rose
And brought Montgom'ry to its close,
      A sandy hill.

And when the rich discovered ore,
So many lured to seek the shore,
      Then Leidesdorff died.
But soon a kind successor came,
Whose friendly acts endeared his name
      On every side.

For who did not regard the man,[9]
When first the tidal wave began
    Its influx here ;
Who unto all, that sought his aid
A kind and generous hand displayed,
    With friendly cheer.

And when a project was begun
To build a church, and have it done
    Without delay ;
A school, or lodge, for any good,
'T was he, who ever foremost stood,
    To aid the way.

This tribute then, we deem in place,
For in the city's weal, we trace,
    His helping hand ;
That in the State's grand progress, too,
The part it took, and had to do,
    Will brightly stand.

And now, that bold aggressive war,
No longer vexed this western shore,
    By sea or land;
The powers at home, proposed a scheme,
To have each month, a mail by steam
    At their command.

But hard it was, to find the man
Of soul so great, to risk a plan,
    That naught assured;
And not till Gotham's son came forth,[10]
The princely merchant of the North,
    Was it secured.

When, thro' his zeal, prompt means were wrought,
Whereby, to reach this idol Port
    And golden land;
Where thousands now are here to-day,
Who 'd not been here, but for the way
    Oped by his hand.

For which they laud him as their friend,
For which the world will e'er commend
　　His vent'rous act ;
And when we praise him for it here,
We 'll hail him as the Pioneer
　　In truth and fact.

But let us turn to other scenes
Where progress now has scarce left means
　　Amidst our rise,　　,
To trace the lines of by-gone days—
With all their charms, and social ways,
　　Save memory's ties.

There, on your left, upon the strand
Amid the piles of drifted sand,
　　That strewed the shore.
A warehouse stood, that in its day,
Was justly called, we well may say,
　　A model store.

Where rolled the tides, so near its base
They scarcely left a foot-path space
    Along its side ;
Which, when blocked up, as often seen,
Gave no spare room to pass between
    The house and tide.

Oft then a launch lay near the shore,
In hailing distance from the store
    The flood to wait ;
And when enabled by the tide
She, from the very warehouse side,
    Embarked her freight.

For then the Steamship's Agent, made
This famous spot, for truck and trade
    His business place ;
Where now, upon the very spot
An iron warehouse fills the lot
    With comely grace.

'T was oft the scene of many a strife
'Twixt parties, who, with rudeness rife
        Enforced their way ;
To be the first to make secure
A homeward passage doubly sure
        For steamer day—

And though it stood upon the shore
A lone attraction, as before
        The rapid change ;
'T is now the centre of the town,
And hid by structures of renown
        That round it range.   .

Still further on, a space beyond
Where once was seen a shallow pond,
        Stood Leidesdorff's store ;
From whence ran out a puny pier,
The first that graced the landing here
        Before the war—

The searching eye met nothing more
Along this unfrequented shore,
     So bleak and bare ;
Till "*Rincon Point*" its craggy bluff
Projected out with boldness rough,
     And visage rare.

Unless it were the "*Happy Vale*,"
That sheltered from the frequent gale,
     Was Cupid's pride ;
Whose groves and walks from day to day,
Were ever thronged with lovers gay
     From far and wide.

For there, the trees and shrubs so green
With foliage rich as e'er was seen
     In Paradise ;
And flowers, too, of brilliant hue
That fostered by the morning dew,
     Did odors rise.

And made it thus a haunt for love,
Whilst Nature there, the cooing dove
  In pairs had sent;
That by their plaintive notes so rare
They might the hallowed place declare
  When Love there went.

It was for festive sports the spot,
Where many a crowd its surfeit got,
  Of joy and glee;
As there they chased dull care away,
From early morn till close of day,
  So light and free.

And now, behold, upon your right,
Near "*Simes's Bank*," friend *Nathan's* site,"
  A grassy mound;
Where stood his house, his mill and store,
With little garden, too, before,
  All fenced around.

And further on, where now doth run
The street called " *Clay*," then just begun,
    Lived *Vioget;*[12]
Whose fancy cottage and saloon
Were ever crowded, morn and noon,
    For billiard play.

The "*Custom House*" and " *Town Hotel*,"
Remain for us to state how well
    Their fate they bore ;
And how they stood, preserved with care,
For years the pride of "*Portsmouth Square*,"
    As gems of yore.

A few more buildings scattered round,
Upon this " *Yerba Buena*" ground,
    Made up the town ;
And near North Beach we yet may find,
The last memento of its kind,
    In lone renown.[13]

PREAMBLE III.

With a parting adieu to the bright
    golden town,
And its fêtes that so endless
    abound ;
We embark on a steamer, whose name
    and renown,
Have extended indeed the
    world round.

For who but remembers the "Senator's"
    fame,
And éclat for the fortune
    she won
When, with crowded saloon, and deck
    too, the same,
She up toward the gold region
    run.

The harvests she gathered were bright
    yellow gold,
Quite enriching her owners
    indeed ;
As o'er the broad basin she
    gallantly roll'd,
And traversed the river
    with speed.

And now, though no longer the river
    she plies,
  But o'er the blue waters
    doth run ;
Yet still her rich harvests continue
    to rise,
  And add to the piles she
    has won.

So, steaming away, we soon traverse
    the bar,
  Gliding on o'er the billows
    so gay ;
Till point after point receding
    afar,
  Brings us close to the end of
    the day.

At length the green hills of Point Pinos
appear,
Rising up like a cloud from
the deep ;
And ere the sun setting, we hail
with a cheer,
Its blanch dunes, where the wild
surges leap.

MONTEREY.

CANTO III.

The pine clad hills of Monterey,
Behold them in their vestment gay,
    Of beauty rare;
There soaring upward toward the skies,
In matchless grandeur as they rise,
    So bright and fair!

Yet ah! how sad to see them harmed,
And so despoiled of all that charmed
    The raptured gaze;
When forests dense their summits crown'd,
And spread their foliage thick around,
    In one dark maze.

Not e'en their beauty could them save,
Nor all the prayers true homage gave,
    To have them spared;
Nor threats of law, nor Lynch alarm,
Could have effect to stay the harm
    The spoiler dared.

He hearkened not, he heeded not,
But hewed away from spot to spot,
    With laughing scorn;
Proclaiming as he bent his way,
" *For this our Government did pay*
    Ye Greasers born ! "

And so, good " *Uncle Sam* " became
A cloak for crime, though not to blame
    For such misdeed;
Whilst here and there, the squatter, too,
Did chuckling sneer, and pay his due,
    With self-same plead.

In truth 't was thus throughout the State,
With waggish rogues, who caught the bait,
    As " *Sam's true kin;* "
As on they went, these rightful heirs,
Whate'er they craved, proclaiming theirs,
    For 't was no sin.

But let us leave this brigand scene,
For one more staid and pure, I ween,
    Of days gone by ;
When peace and plenty bless'd the land,
And hearts content went hand in hand,
    With scarce a sigh.

For in those days it was that came,
Those goodly men of pious fame,
    To teach the way ;
When yet the woods and hills around,
With wild beasts' howl did loud resound,
    Both night and day.

When oft-times then, old grizzly made
His seaside stroll, to dauntless wade
　　Within the sea ;
Or feast upon some carcass there,
Of stranded whale, or some such fare,
　　That there might be.

When at noonday he'd plunge the wave,
The stormy billows fierce to brave,
　　The old folks say ;
And dashing through them gain the shore,
Where habit led him, oft before,
　　In quest of prey.

Beyond these scenes we thus portray,
Which form the outskirts of the bay,
　　A ruin lies ;
Of rough-hewn stone, whose relics tell
Its once proud state, and also, well
　　The spot descries.

It is a charming place, and proves
That he who lived there liked its groves,
    And had good taste;
For search the region all around,
Another spot could scarce be found
    So truly chaste.

'T was there progression first appeared.
That paved the way which culture cheered
    In after age;
And many a relic must decay,
Ere all its charms be swept away,
    From Nature's page.

The little Church, so lonely left,
Though now, by Time, of much bereft,
    That gave it life;
Yet proudly stands a monument
To those whose lives were freely lent
    In days of strife.

In primal times a martial square
Did shield its shrine from outward care
    And hostile fear;
When clank of arms and rolling drum,
With piercing fife and warriors' hum,
    Gave constant cheer.

For many a Spanish hero, then,
With half a thousand loyal men,
    Did guard its walls;
When scarce a day, but joy and glee,
Its hours would end, with hearts so free,
    In routs and balls.

With music too! the light guitar,
That gently touched, was dearer far,
    By maiden's hand;
Whose silvered voice, in alto clear,
Revealed sweet love in strains most dear,
    From Castile's land.

Thus briskly time did pass away,
Forever free and ever gay,
  With song and dance ;
For naught but pleasure then did reign,
Whilst love of home, and faith to Spain,
  Did joy enhance.

And though but slow the town progressed,
It here and there, at length possessed
  Some thriving spots ;
Yet scattered so upon the green,
Their cosy huts were faintly seen,
  Like little dots.

But, strange to say, not one betrayed
The slightest taste for floral aid,
  Their grounds to charm ;
For scarce a tree or shrub was there,
Save nature's growth, that void of care,
  Had 'scaped from harm.

And so it was, till other hands
Had come afar, from distant lands,
          These dearths to share ;
When soon a thriving garden plot,
Made bright each comer's homestead lot,
          With flowers rare.

But see where now so sightly stands
Yon rustic mound, whose site commands
          The town and bay ;
Where once the Royal Standard waved,
And where bold valor fearless braved,
          The savage fray.

For 't was the fortress in its day,
Erected there to guard the way,
          To Christian light ;
And long it did a shelter yield,
To those who then the cross did wield
          For ends so bright.

But more remote its cannon drove,
A private squadron from the cove,¹⁴
    Where they would land ;
Repelling prompt their bold attack,
With such effect that forced them back,
    To join their band.

And though their bark seemed much impaired,
They put to sea, and boldly dared,
    To risk the main ;
Full eager, too, to leave to spot,
Where pluck and skill had foiled their plot,
    And hope for gain.

Since which grand feat, so val'rous won,
Its rampart scarce has fired a gun,
    Save when for sport ;
Or sign to guide some lonely bark,
That sought at night, when late and dark,
    To gain the port.

Unless we cite rebellion's feat,
When fierce incensed to warlike heat
 The Creole rose ;
And ere the town its slumbers raised,
The fortress seized, and from it blazed
 Upon their foes.

A spacious lawn that cheers the bank,
Reveals the spot where many a prank
 Full pleasure won ;
Where oft the *merienda* bade
Both old and young, of every grade,
 To join its fun.

At which they danced and sang away,
With mirthful glee and sportive play,
 Till day had ceased ;
While not a soul of social heart,
Who in the merry fête took part,
 But seemed well pleased.

E'en now, as then, the grounds remain,
With many a wreck that long hath lain
        Strewed o'er the shore ;
Of odds and ends of divers kind,
Which all so freely bring to mind,
        Those freaks of yore.

But ah ! there's yet a dearer spot,
Which no true hearts hath yet forgot,
        That claims our pen ;
To tell how there a Patriarch
Doth lie entomb'd, without a mark,
        The place to ken.

It is the one o'er yonder hill,
Where many a trace remaineth still
        Of auld lang syne ;
Where once the jolly Friar laughed
With full content, as pleased he quaffed
        His ruby wine.

This ancient site, or Mission post,
So long attractive on the coast,
 Still holds its spell ;
For there the sainted "*Serra*" lies,[15]
And many a Father, good and wise,
 Of whom they tell ;

Whom oft historic pages praise
As men who did their voices raise
 In holy pride ;
Whose works and acts the critic ne'er,
We hope, will dare to treat unfair
 Or aught deride.

Go ask the aged Creole now
How fared he, when, with lowly bow,
 He craved their aid ;
And hear him say, with downcast look,
"*Though richer now, I'd rather brook*
 The needy jade !"

Go ask the voyager how he bore
The rugged pastime then on shore,
   And hear *his* voice :
"*Though now there's comfort all around,*
To have it, as it then was found,
   Would be my choice !"

PREAMBLE IV.

Resounding aloud from the hills
    that arise
O'er the scene which encircles
    the bay,
Booms the peal of a cannon, whose
    re-echo dies,
Like a thunder-clap rolling
    its way.

'Tis the signal for parting — our
labor is done ;
The ship's anchor hangs fast to
her side ;
So it's ho ! for the ocean again
now to run,
And on its proud billows
to ride.

Swift onward we journey, enjoying
the night,
Now so placid, so gentle
and free,
That scarce a white ripple appears
to the sight,
So smooth is the beauteous
sea.

When morning appears, we are close
to the shore,
Rolling swiftly along, blithe
and gay ;
Till at length "*Point Concepcion*" abaft
us soon bore,
And its vision fast fading
away.

Anon, we beheld o'er the caps
of the land,
That precede the first glimpse of
a town,
Two lofty church towers, whose aspect,
so grand,
Quite betokened a place of
renown.

But distance, we find, on arriving,
 had given
An enchantment indeed to
 the view ;
For, instead of a city, with kirks to
 enliven,
E'en the houses were scattered
 and few.

SANTA BARBARA.

CANTO IV.

Yon mountain range that soars on high,[16]
Whose towering peaks salute the sky
  In Alps-like form ;
Did Fremont pass, one darksome night,
And brave the dangers of its height
  'Mid howling storm.

When down the bold and cragged steep
His gallant steeds did wildly leap
  O'er cleft and rock ;
And crushed to death were piled up found
A frightful heap and ghastly mound,
  The sight to shock.

And oh ! what tales of blood are told,
Of murder there, most foul and bold,
    By villain done,
For vengeance, or for paltry gain,
That, to recount, would render pain
    To more than one.

For many a victim there doth lay,
Now mould'ring in his home of clay,
    Whose fate is hid ;
Whilst here, within the very town,
His slayer stalks with fearless frown,
    The crowd amid.

Yet brighter scenes the landscape shows,
More genial, too, good Heaven knows,
    The heart to cheer ;
That bring to mind those blissful days,
Of by-gone times and guileless ways,
    To memory dear.

Behold, where yon lone Mission stands,
Amidst its hills and rolling lands,
    So stately seen ;
Whose crumbling relics, scattered round,
Evince that once 't was thriving found,
    And rich hath been.

And see its thrifty gardens, too,
With flowing fountains, pure as dew,
    And works of art ;
And stony church, whose walls within,
So hang with scenes depicting sin,
    They daunt the heart.

Fit scenes, indeed, the savage mind
To tantalize, and firmly bind
    To moral acts ;
For clearly thus, it sees portrayed
The end of sin, by art displayed,
    Like glaring facts.

And now, behold, all bright to view,
The little town, and fortress, too,
    Half hid by trees ;
With here and there a gaysome spot,
Of garden fair, or verdant plot,
    To cheer and please.

The buildings, few and far between,
Though low, present a comely mien,
    When seen aloof ;
Whose milk-white walls made still more fair,
In contrast with the ruddy glare
    Of each tiled roof.

And on the strand whăt sights we see,
In rompish scenes of joy and glee,
    With mirthful play ;
Where boatmen toil with jolly song,
And lift their voices loud and strong,
    So blithe and gay.

Indeed, 't was once a merry sight
To watch their pranks from morn till night,
    So full of charm ;
As through the surf they burdens bore,
And placed them safe upon the shore,
    E'er free from harm.

This busy spot the Indian sought,
And often here his offspring brought,
    In days when free ;
To brave the waves in sportive play,
Or boldly dare, with hearts e'er gay,
    The ruffled sea.

And often, too, he would resort
To where then stood the barrack fort,
    To play at ball ;
And wager deep, to thus enhance,
As e'er the case, in games of chance,
    The zeal of all.

The barracks formed a spacious square,
And then a guard was stationed there,
    To check surprise ;
For yet the Indian, wild and bold,
Sought oftentimes, we have been told,
        In vain to rise.

For records of the Mission tell
How once he boldly did rebel
        Against the Crown ;
And, fearless, sought to drive away
The royal corps which then held sway
        Within the town;

When all the troop of mounted horse
Was prompt despatched, in ample force,
        And valiant led ;
That marching up the Mission hill,
So charged, with truly martial skill,
        The Indians fled.

Just then, howe'er, in merry peals,
The Parish bell loud toll'd for meals,
    When ceased the fight ;
And special orders to retreat
Were followed up with zeal replete
    And eager flight.

The dinner o'er, the troop returned,
To find the Mission sacked and burned,
    And Indians gone ;
And so with this a victory claimed,
With ne'er a horse or soldier maimed
    Throughout the morn.

In these rude times, when fearless came
Those gallant knights of brilliant fame,
    From Castile's lands ;
When Christian conquest yet was young,
And converts rare were made among
    The savage bands —

Came one, who vowed to faithful serve,[17]
With holy zeal and steadfast nerve,
　　The righteous cause;
And ever constant to fulfill
The mandate of his monarch's will,
　　His creed and laws.

Which vow, with firmness he observed,
And from it ne'er had even swerved,
　　In thought or way;
And faithful to his liege command,
Amidst the trials of the land,
　　He did not stray.

As chieftain, friend or private cit.,
In grand concourse, or scenes of wit,
　　His talent shone;
And bounteous to the needy poor,
To all he gave, who sought his door
　　Their wants to moan.

As Christian, sure the church can claim
But few who bore so fair a name
    Within its fold ;
And long her prayers will cease to flow
Ere she forgets to justly show
    These facts of old.

And as he lived, he calmly died,
His country's friend—his people's pride,
    And is no more ;
Yet " *Guerra's* " name shall lasting stand,
A record of his long-loved land,
    Till Time is o'er.

Among the isles that skirt the shore,[18]
Was one oft sought in days of yore
    For pelts and oil ;
Till constant raids of hunters there
Quite left them stripp'd and almost bare
    Of all such spoil.

'T is said that once a feud they made,
And 'gainst the native bared the blade
    In bloody fight ;
When death's destruction proved the end
Of nearly all who would defend
    Their homes and right.

Indeed, the *Russian Codiack*
An onslaught made that long did rack
    The public mind ;
As sadly told, the tidings went,
And o'er the wide-spread world were sent
    To tell mankind.

In modern times, some sportsmen sought
This self-same spot for rural sport
    And hunting cheer ;
When, strolling o'er the dreary shore,
They spied a group, which fled before
    With haste and fear.

Amazed, the sportsmen gave it chase,
And followed up a toilsome race
    Along the strand ;
Until, within a half-hid nook,
The fugitives were overtook,
    And bade to stand.

One aged chief of humble mien,
With three rude dames, one, scarce sixteen,
    The group combined ;
Who, crouching low upon the sand,
Obeyed at once the stern command,
    With hearts resigned.

Their fears howe'er were quickly quelled,
And dread of harm was soon dispelled
    By change to glee ;
For, uncontrolled, they did consent
Their home to leave, with heart's content,
    And cross the sea.

So anxious now to reach the main,
The party sought the launch to gain
        Ere closed the day ;
But on the way, as blithe they went,
The elder matron did relent
        And stole away.

They sailed howe'er, and left her there
Alone, her gloomy fate to bear,
        Though 't was unkind;
And rolling o'er the swelling sea
Their little bark sped onward free
        Before the wind.

Unharmed, they passed the channel o'er
And reached e'er morn, their destined shore,
        San Pedro bay;
When landed safe, upon the beach
They soon set off, the town to reach
        Without delay.

'T is quite enough for us to say,
They reached the town, and spent each day
    In festal glee ;
But rash excess, and change of fare,
For these rude dames so free to share,
    Did not agree.

Alas ! they died and left behind
The poor old chief, whose care-worn mind
    Ne' er ceased to mourn ;
Who, wandering sad from place to place,
At length was missed, without a trace,
    To tell where gone.

As time went by, he was forgot,
Till accident revealed the spot
    Beside the shore ;
Where, crush'd with sorrow, he had strayed,
And there, a maniac, betrayed
    The grief he bore.

Lo ! there he sat from day to day,
E'er gazing o'er the channel way,
        Perchance to gain
A glimpse of home beyond the sea —
Of that lone isle, where once so free,
        He lord did reign.

But fate decreed he never more,
Should know again that cherished shore
        His heart did crave ;
For on the deep one morn was found
His floating corse, with sea-birds crown'd,
        That told his grave.

'T was thought, whilst gazing on the deep,
Stretch'd on the cliff, he went to sleep
        Too near its side ;
And dreaming of that long-loved isle,
With on his lips perhaps a smile,
        He fell and died.

The end was thus of poor "*Black Hawk,*"
Of whom the tourists oft may talk,
    And tell a tale;
And drop a tear, in memory, too,
For him and those who e'er did rue
        Their vent'rous sail.

Some eighteen years had rolled away,
Since that eventful, doleful day
    We here recall;
When she, who on the isle remained,
Was hither brought, and entertained
        With warmth by all.

The change, howe'er its mischief wrought,
And soon 'twas known she here was brought
    To sink and die;
For human kindness could not save
This *lone* and *last one* from the grave
        Where she doth lie.

PREAMBLE V.

With a parting salute, we are soon
    underway,
O'er the ocean again, now
    to roam ;
Where its frolicsome billows unceasingly
    play, .
As they scatter around us
    their foam.

And as we steam onward, we view
  with delight,
Where the mountains recede from
  the shore,
The evergreen gardens fresh, blooming
  and bright,
With their little blanch'd cabins
  before.

'Tis "*La Carpenteria,*" and the famous
  " *Rincon,*"
Both a nice little drive from
  the town ;
Where many a fête hath imparted
  a tone,
And success to their name and
  renown.

So that parties oft visit their shores
    to obtain
  When the waters flow back from
    the land,   '
A repast from the mussels its shallows
    contain,
  And that cling to the rocks on
    the sand.

A few leagues beyond this, we see
    near the shore,
  What remains of a once thrifty
    Mission ;
Disclosing now ruins, where grand
    structures before,
  Paraded in fine
    exhibition.

Alas! all such stations are fading
          away,
As their wealth and their power
          have gone ;
And sad is the picture their relics
          portray,
Now crumbling to dust, and
          forlorn.

On our right stands the island called
          "*Anacapap*,"
A mere cluster of rocks, and
          no more ;
Where the "*Scott*" laid her timbers, within
          a deep gap,
As she went with a crash on
          the shore.

Anon, like a cloud, rising up
  from the mist,
 Far away in the distance
  appear,
San Pedro's rude hillocks, whose features
  enlist
 A distrust in their shelter
  and cheer.

But gliding along we soon enter
  the bay,
 Running close within hail of
  the land,
And ere the ship's anchor rests fast
  in the clay,
 Her freight agent from shore, is
  on hand.

Who, ever efficient, is ever
prepared
For his patrons, whenever
they call;
And his coaches are decent and nicely
repaired,
With comfort and roomage
for all.

So, taking our leave of the captain,
we pass
To the lighter, which takes us
away;
Yet not, till together, we join
in a glass,
And first drink to his health, as
they say.

For who did not fancy Tom Seely
    as skip,
Or as friend and companion
    on shore;
For a more genial sailor ne'er handled
    a ship,
Nor traversed the ocean
    before.

At length, having landed, we scale
    the bluff-way,
Excavated adroitly with
    care;
When a Postal politely invites
    us to pay
At a station, near by, the
    coach fare.

But time will permit us without
        much delay,
A slight glance at the neighboring
        shore ;
So we'll glean what we can of its charms,
        while we may,
To append to the Past, as
        before.

SAN PEDRO.

CANTO V.

Lone, cheerless spot, and desert shore,
Where surges roll, and ceaseless roar,
    So dull and drear;
Whose hills reach far beyond the sight,
Till fading, like the evening light,
    They disappear.

Lo! there San Juan's tall peaks arise,
Upheaving toward the lofty skies,
    And crown'd with snow;
Whilst prairies green that intervene,
Make up the grandeur of the scene,
    Which lies below.

The time was once, when o'er this space,
Like little dots, the eye might trace,
    O'er vale and mound
The countless herds of grazing stock,
Upon a soil, where ne'er a rock
    Disturbed the ground.

And roaming wild, might then be seen,
In playful mood, and lively mien,
    The gallant steed ;
Who, o'er the plains would swiftly bound,
And sniff the air, as o'er the ground
    He pranced with speed.

And then the creek within the bay,
A sight revealed, from day to day,
    The eye to please ;
Of drowsy seals, in scattered bands,
Whose thousands basked upon the sands
    In tranquil ease.

A rugged ridge called "Dead Man's Isle,"
Was oft the spot where they did pile
    E'en to its top;
And lying there, stretched in the sun,
Till thorough dried, they one by one
    Would downward drop.

When quite alive would be the sea,
As round the isle unchecked and free
    They sportive bayed;
Whose barking sounds did loud resound
Within the Port, for miles around,
    As there they played.

For then, as monarchs of the bay,
These creatures held unbroken sway
    With naught to fear;
Till came a roving, murd'rous band,
Whose galley, coasting near the land,
    Sought shelter here.

When fierce destruction then began,
That ended not till savage man
  Had laid them waste ;
And now 't is rare that one appears,
Unless compelled by modern fears
  From harm to haste.

At length some zealous trader sought
To barter here, the goods he brought
  With wonted cheer ;
And oped a trade for after age
To follow up, and duly wage
  ⁃ From year to year.

For then throughout this far-famed coast
San Pedro's Port could proudly boast
  The largest trade ;
And greatest share of exports, too ,
Of hides and pelts, with furs a few,
  That then were made.

PREAMBLE VI.

Now the coaches were waiting for
    orders to start,
With their horses quite prancing
    and gay ;
So we scarcely get seated, ere bounding
    we part
And are racing along the
    highway.

The reason for haste is, the public
well know,
They're running a strong
competition ;
And speed is their maxim, wherever
they go,
To outrival and beat
opposition.

So fleet do we travel, we soon
reach the plains,
More or less than ten leagues from
the sea ;
When the distance before us most cheerfully
wanes,
As we chit-chat so friendly
and free.

A loquacious gent, half reclined
  on his seat,
 Ever anxious the Yankees
  to bore,
Related the tale of an ill-timed
  retreat,
 Which occurred in the Mexican
  War.

'T was the one that recounts how the
  Yankees, one day,
 In their zeal and fresh hope for
  renown,
From their war-ship fierce landed in battle
  array,
 And set off to lay siege to
  the town.

Their forces, he told us, were met
    on the way,
By a squadron of native
    dragoons,
Who, well mounted on chargers both
    prancing and gay,
Were advancing in gallant
    platoons.

A little brass cannon much glory
    did gain
As it mowed down the ranks of
    their foe ;
And forced it to turn and fall back
    on the plain
Far away from disaster
    and woe.

The gist of the tale is, when the
    Yankees retired,
In disordered retreat from
    the field ;
The natives down-hearted, their last
    shot had fired,
And were only just ready
    to yield.

The story so given, spread laughter
    around,
As the gent it with mirth did
    unfold ;
And we thought, if 't were truthful, it
    certainly crown'd
All the feats of the war that
    are told.

Had the Yankees continued their march
for the town,
Without care for any
collision,
They might have succeeded and gained
a renown,
Instead of this slur of
derision.

Ascending a rising, distinctly
we saw,
For some leagues the fine country
around,
With its lofty dark mountains that shoot
up before,
And its prairies where cattle
abound.

A glimpse, too, we had, of the nice
    little town,
  Though partially hid by
-     the trees,
Where its gardens and vineyards of well-
    known renown,
  So adorn it, and charmingly
    please.

The summit descended, we race
    o'er the ground,
  Now so level and smooth as
    it lay ;
On each side the bright flowers, fresh
    blooming around,
  Adding charm to the scenes on
    the way.

In the Spring of the year the whole country
abounds
In its flowers, the choicest
of hue,
When scarce then a spot can be found
o'er its grounds,
But a garden presents to
to the view.

A short distance further, brings us safe
into town,
Where we halt at the house of
a friend,
And alighting, rejoice, as we quickly
leap down,
That we've got to our long journey's
end.

LOS ANGELES.

CANTO VI.

—— ——

" El Pueblo de los Angeles,"
Indeed the town of Angels is,
    Of beauty rare ;
And t' is a spot that gives delight,
That fills the soul with rapture bright
    And visions fair !

Its walks, its rides, its hills and dales,
Its grassy plains, and fertile vales,
    With flowers bloom,
Whose blossoms bright, sweet odors rise,
And fragrant greet the fost'ring skies
    In rich perfume.

What joy ! what gay content was here,
With scenes so chaste, and charms so dear,
    'Mong hearts so free ;
When irksome toil, and gloomy care
Gave place to pleasure everywhere
    In mirth and glee !

With homes thus blest, their wants were few,
Of things abroad, they scarcely knew,
    Or gave a thought ;
But well content with what they had,
They ask'd no more their hearts to glad,
    Nor wished for aught.

For with a clime so soft and mild
They lived along, from care beguiled,
    In constant health ;
Their grazing flocks on every side.
Enhancing e'er their worldly pride,
    And source of wealth.

Thus time went by, from day to day,
In social sport and constant play,
    With song and dance ;
From twilight eve 'till early dawn,
Within the cot, or on the lawn,
    In blissful trance.

And on some special gala day,
Then hundreds came from far away
    To join its cheer ;
When old and young would, mounted, dare
To taunt the bull, or savage bear,
    Devoid of fear.

So, deck'd in all their gayest pride,
Each horseman bold did gallant ride
    With dext'rous skill ;
And there before his love display
Such feats that naught could him repay,
    Save her good-will.

But woe to him, from his adored
If by mischance his horse got gored,
     Or he got thrown ;
For either fault would quite suffice
To cause dismissal in a trice
     With scornful frown.

'T was rare howe'er, or scarce was heard,
That such mishap had e'er occurred
     To man or horse ;
For o'er the world from East to West,
As riders they were deemed the best,
     On turf or course.

The children, too, could famous ride,
And three or four would sometimes stride
     A gallant steed ;
The youngest in the middle placed,
When o'er the town they wildly raced,
     With scarce a heed.

But ah ! alas, such times have fled,
And though grand wealth now reigns instead
  To comfort life ;
Yet, with the change, untimely came
A host of rogues, whose vicious fame
  Brought constant strife.

For here they found a home for vice
Wherein to sow with cards and dice
  Their venomed deeds ;
Among a race who rude withal
Too easy bent to mischief's call
  And grasped its seeds.

But later, theft and murder came,
Both followed up with equal fame
  From time to time ;
Till scarce a day, but three or four
Were murdered found, and sometimes more,
  By growth of crime.

For such a vile and noxious set
Of midnight thieves, was never met
    The world around ;
And cut-throats, too, who dealt in blood,
Whose fiendish acts, alas, did flood
    And steep the ground.

They were " Sonora's " vilest fruits,
And direst pests, that, like fierce brutes,
    On blood would feast ;
Whose dreadful crimes have scarcely left
A home extant, that's not bereft
    Of friends, at least.

But, as the time at length progressed,
Such fiendish acts were prompt suppressed
    By strength of arm ;
When " Sonorensic " malice fled
And left its haunts with anxious dread
    And wild alarm.

Since which these lands, thus purg'd of crime,
Have merit gained from time to time
  As culture came ;
And now, indeed, for leagues around,
With labor rife, are thriving found
  And have great fame.

Far o'er the hills, we may behold,
Still central in its open wold
  A remnant yet
Of olden time, whose blighted fame
And sad decline must surely claim
  The world's regret.

For there once stood a grand domain [19]
Within its wide-spread fertile plain
  Like some proud queen ;
With garden groves and vineyards fair
Whose varied fruits, both choice and rare,
  Were charming seen.

But like its consorts in the State,
She too, has shared the grievous fate
        They sadly bore ;
And thus her Indian convert here,
Compelled by want to disappear,
        Is seen no more.

An index sad, of modern days,
Which serves to prove in many ways
        The maxim true ;
That where the Saxon foot doth go,
It carries with it waste and woe
        For them to rue.

But ah ! indeed, 't is Nature's course
The ever-certain, willful source
        Whence comes the blow ;
And is the destined fate they bear
Which human aid can ne'er repair
        Nor stay its woe.

For culture must enforce its way,
With onward march from day to day
 Where rudeness lies ;
And so the Red Man, here to-day,
To modern progress must give way,
 Though thus he *dies !*

PREAMBLE VII.

But let us return to the town's
    merry haunts
And its scenes ever happy
    and gay ;
Where there's comfort and pastime to
    gladden the wants
Of the trav'ler who ventures
    this way.

Beside the bright eye of the native
    brunette,
That out-dazzles the gems she
    may wear,
There is love in the Pike's to tease
    and to fret,
And a mildness to soften
    dull care.

There are vineyards and orchards and
    gardens and fields
That embellish the village
    around ;
With the sweetest of grape that abundantly
    yields
And other choice fruits that
    abound.

The roads through the suburbs are
  charming indeed,
 With their little scant streams on
  each side,
Where the bright verdant hedges though
  covered with weed,
 Add much to their fame far
  and wide.

The country surrounding has greatly
  progressed,
 Giving life to its precincts
  around ;
And the Mormon intrusion, so lately
  suppressed
 Doth now with attraction
  abound.

There's the range of Santana, and vale
of San Juan,
Far away from the skirts of
the town,
So thriving with plenty, they must
be anon
Grand places of wealth and
renown.

In fact, the whole country is blessed
with success,
And its people are happy
and gay,
For, without molestations to grieve
and oppress,
They have nothing to hamper
their way.

So thus we will leave them and haste
    to the strand,
  Once again to resume from
    the sea
A view of the sights which encompass
    the land
  And give vim to their charms, gay
    and free.

Suffice it, that safe we arrive
    at the bay,
  Where the steamer lies ready
    to part ;
So quickly embarking, we are prompt
    under way,
  With a speed that gives joy to
    the heart.

For soon, the bold bluff of " Point
Loma " appears,
As the hill of " San Pedro "
grows dim,
With the coast line so near us, that
often with cheers,
We are hailed by the groups on
its brim.

These greetings so cheerful, were all
that we met,
To attract and divert on
the way ;
And yet their dull sameness gave naught
to regret,
For with music, we pass'd off
the day.

At length a bell warned us of something
at hand,
And the steamer soon slackened
her way ;
So we hied to the deck, whence we saw
'twas the land,
Whose surroundings we came to
survey.

SAN DIEGO.

CANTO VII.

All hail, most blest and sacred spot,[20]
On which it was famed Serra's lot,
    Rome's cross to raise ;
And on a lonesome, dreary strand,
To consecrate, with hallowed hand,
    The Host we praise !

For there, his first "Grand Mass" was said,
In offering to the great God-head,
    His work to bless,
That by God's holy will decreed
The Christian conquest might proceed
    With true success.

And there it was, he first began
To soothe the ways of Pagan man,
    A savage race ;
Yet ah ! what dangers did he dare
Their hearts to tame, so they might share
    The convert's grace.

What wants, what cares and risks he bore !
An exile to this heathen shore
    Where darkness lay ;
With naught to cheer or charm the mind,
Nor e'en a shelter from the wind,
    To smooth his way.

And yet, withal, he faltered not,
But with a will that's not forgot,
    Urged on his way ;
By smiles and gifts and friendly bribes,
That gained him ground among the tribes
    From day to day.

Till, by degrees, his station grew,
As eager round it, converts drew
    To join his creed ;
And with it learn, though rudely taught,
Such useful arts, as he best thought
    They most did need.

By which their huts were better framed,
Their lands were tilled and flocks were tamed
    O'er vale and hill ;
And many a fabric yet doth stand
A leading wonder in the land
    To prove their skill.

As time elapsed and years passed o'er,
At length arose upon the shore
    A little town ;
Whose modest structures scattered round
Were sheltered 'neath a fortress mound
    Of old renown.

And one, the most imposing seen,[21]
Of plain design and humble mien,
    We will portray ;
For there a wealthy Don did dwell
Whose heart, the living town can tell,
    Was kind and gay.

Where scarce a night, but dance and song
The fleeting hours did chase along
    In mirth and glee ;
When old and young, from far and wide,
E'er gathered round, on every side,
    The sport to see.

For always free these pastimes were
To rich and poor, who chose to share
    The social call ;
When gaily dressed, both prompt would hie
Each other's grace and charms to vie
    At every ball.

And there would grace and beauty meet
Their nets to spread, some swain to cheat
    Whose heart was bland ;
And gaily lead him on to love,
As round the hall they brisk did move,
    Joined hand in hand.

But of the beauty then in town,
None could compare, we sure must own,
    Throughout the land,
With that which graced our friend's domain,
Whose gentle sweetness e'er did gain
    All hearts command.

And who that now recalls those nights,
Those ever-charming, joyous sights,
    The peasants' balm,—
But feels a sadness on his brow,
That such delights no longer now
    Are here to charm.

They have dispersed ! A stranger's sway
Such rural treats has swept away
    And left behind
A blank instead, with naught to please,
A gloomy scene, to chill and freeze
    The gaysome mind.

Two humble dwellings, side by side "
That stood for years the village pride
    Are standing now,
In which two gallant sailors dwelt
Whose hearts in friendship ever felt
    A kindred glow.

Like brothers they were bound in love,
And in their acts each zealous strove
    His love to vie,
That bated not, nor even waived
Through all the changes they had braved
    Till both did die.

And as they lived, so since they died
They have been neighbors side by side,
    And tenants are
Within a ruin'd church-yard laid
Where many a kith and kin have strayed
    To lisp a prayer.

Two simple slabs, their names impart
That tell the day they did depart
    This world's career ;
And he who stops to read the fact
Will breathe a sigh while in the act,
    And drop a tear.

Not far beyond, upon a green,
A simple structure may be seen,
    With latticed fence,
Where lie reposed, those valiant men
Who lost their lives within a glen
    Some leagues from hence.

Poor victims of an oversight
Which history claims as something bright
    And worthy fame,
Though here 'twas deemed a foul defeat,
And caused by leaders incomplete,
    Who were to blame.

At least, 'tis said by those who know
That ere was struck the fatal blow,
    Had order reigned,
The battle lost, might have been won,
And they, the victors, made to run
    The field so stained.

But let this pass ! Come view the strand
On which the Pioneers did land
    In days of yore ;
That modern progress scarce has changed
In aught that then around it ranged
    And cheered the shore.

A row of wooden shanties stand
Upon the margin of the land
        Along the beach ;
Where here and there, some launch or hulk
Makes up the vision seen in bulk,
        Within our reach.

'Twas here the early trader brought
The produce he with patience sought
        From mart to mart,
That long lay stored with zealous care,
Until for home he did prepare.
        With gladsome heart.

Then truly 'twas a busy sight
To see the strand from morn till night
        Alive with cheer !
For when a ship was homeward bound,
What merry shouts did then resound
        Afar and near !

Beyond these sights we thus portray
A rustic fort preserves the bay
        Secure and free,
From outward foes and contraband,
That oftentimes disturb the land
        And neighboring sea.

And so with this the past is told—
Whose early days and times of gold
        Have had their charm;
Yet ere we part we fain would crave
The Critic's friendly aid to save
        Our Muse from harm.

NOTES.

(1) The rivers of Sacramento and San Joaquin, whose twin-like streams, side by side, uniting at their mouths, created Suisun Bay, and passing through the Straits of Carquinez into the magnificent basin of San Pablo formed a copartnership with that of San Francisco, and finally passed out through the Golden Gate into the deep bosom of the Pacific Ocean. It has been said by the early historical writers that the bay of San Francisco originally extended far south over the valley of San Jose toward the Tulares, hence the legend of the aborigines describing a lake of grand dimensions, whose waters escaped through an opening created by some unknown revulsion of nature.

(2) The writer alludes to that band of holy missionaries, headed by their venerated president, Friar Junipero Serra, who, under the auspices and protection of the Spanish Government, in 1775, commenced their great work of Christianizing and civilizing the numerous tribes of Indians then inhabiting the northern portion of California,—that is, from San Diego north—at this period a region almost entirely unknown to the civilized world.

(3) Foreign trade was almost exclusively American, confined to trading ships from Boston, Mass., principally by the mercantile houses of Bryant & Sturgis and William Appleton & Co., who, for twenty years, engrossed the entire trade, with the exception of a few outside adventurers, with an occasional ship, also, from Lima, and now and then an expedition from the Sandwich Islands.

(4) General John A. Sutter, a Swiss gentleman, came to this country in 1839, and soon after his arrival, by permission

of the local authorities at Monterey, he established a trading post not far from the present city of Sacramento, which served as a kind of frontier protection to the newly acquired ranchos of the north, which had suffered much from depredations of the unfriendly Indians. By his activity and good management he drew around him a sufficient force of the friendly natives to enable him to erect his grand stronghold, called Sutter's Fort, which held quite a formidable position at the commencement of the war between Mexico and the United States. At this period he made himself serviceable on many occasions to the United States Government, which was duly acknowledged by the authorities in Washington.

(5) The war alluded to was the one between Mexico and the United States, which culminated by the acquisition and annexation of California to the latter, by right of conquest and purchase.

(6) It was the wide-famed Vigilance Committee, so talked of, pro and con, whose acts, though illegal, were successful in ridding the land of a pest of scoundrels and villains who infested it and bade defiance to its laws and authorities.

(7) The residence of Jacob P. Leese, who came to this country overland, via New Mexico, and reached Los Angeles December, 1833, where he took up his residence for a short time, and then proceeded north to San Francisco, where he married Miss Rosalia Vallejo. After the change of government, in 1849, he went to Monterey, since which his family has made that place its permanent home.

(8) Captain William A. Leidesdorff came to this country as Master of the schooner Juliana, owned by John Coffin Jones, Esq., a resident of Santa Barbara, and reached here in June, 1841. Some time afterward he resigned his commission and took up his residence in San Francisco, where he remained until his death, in 1848.

(9) William D. M. Howard arrived here in 1839 on board the ship California (Captain Arthur), and soon after, by permission, he left the ship at San Pedro and took up his residence

with Don Abel Stearns, then a merchant in Los Angeles. He went home to the United States, via Mexico, in 1840, and returned again to this coast in 1842 as assistant supercargo with Captain Arthur on board the ship California, under the patronage of the house of B. T. Read & Co., of Boston. He continued to receive occasional consignments for several years from his friends in Boston, making San Francisco his headquarters, when, in 1849, he made a visit East to his native land, where he became sick, and soon returned to California to die in his princely residence at San Mateo, and was buried in the little stone chapel to which he had so liberally contributed toward its construction.

(10) William H. Aspinwall, who was the first to introduce steam navigation on the Northern Pacific Coast, having contracted with the Government at Washington for the transportation of the U. S. mail across the Isthmus of Panama, thence by water to San Francisco by a line of steamers, the first of which, the California, reached her destination in February, 1849.

(11) Nathan Spear first visited this coast from the Sandwich Islands in 1823, and some years afterward he came to Monterey, where he remained but a short time, and then proceeded to San Francisco, where he located permanently. His place of business was on the corner of Montgomery and Clay streets.

(12) John Vioget came to this country in 1837 and located in San Francisco, where he kept a billiard and drinking saloon on Clay street, about half way between Montgomery and Kearny streets. He was a surveyor by profession, and laid out the original plan of San Francisco, extending to Market street. He was from one of the old towns in Switzerland, which probably accounts for the narrow and contracted character of many of the streets so common here.

(13) This was the residence of La Señora Briones, who, in olden times, as a favor did all the washing required by the numerous vessels that visited la Yerba Buena, for which, at that period, the now called North Beach bore the cognomen of " Washerwoman's Bay."

(14) This was a patriot vessel-of-war, under command of one Buchard, who, after his departure from Monterey, proceeded southward and anchored off the *Refugio* Rancho, located about half way between Point Concepcion and the Presidio of Santa Barbara, where a force landed and destroyed almost entirely the little settlement which they found there, and then continued on their course south, until they reached *La Mission de San Juan Capistrano.* Here they disembarked a force which, after ransacking and damaging to some considerable extent, and consuming the wine and little niceties of the old Friars, they returned to their ship in good time to escape being made prisoners by an armed force, which had been sent up from San Diego to protect the Mission.

(15) Padre Junipero Serra, President of the Missionary Department, who died in Monterey and was buried at Carmelo, where, for a long period, the place of his interment was unknown. Recently, however, proofs were ascertained of its locality, and means were taken to substantiate the fact by further investigations, which were successful.

(16) Gen. John C. Fremont came to this country in 1846 as the "Pathfinder," and his first movement was in favor of declaring California independent, and took part in what was called the raising of the Bear Flag in Sonoma. He was prominent in many of the subsequent difficulties which occurred here, until at length they subsided from the entire subjection of the country to the American forces. After the declaration of peace and the admission of California into the Union as a State, he and the Hon. William M. Gwin were elected the first representatives to the Government at Washington. In his intercourse with the native Californians he made himself popular, and they would have been glad to have had him successful in his attempt at Sonoma to establish a free and independent government.

(17) Don José de la Guerra, an native of Novales, Spain, who came to the City of Mexico, and there entered the service of the Government of Spain as a lieutenant, and came to this country in 1802. He was stationed at Monterey, and afterward

appointed Comandante of the Presidio at Santa Barbara. Subsequently he was elected to represent California in the Congress of Mexico, to which place he repaired, where he arrived too late to take his seat, as it had already been taken by his *suplente*, so he returned and resumed his position as Comandante, which he retained for some years, when he retired to private life.

(18) The Island of San Nicholas, which, like its neighboring isles, was once populated, until, from frequent disturbances by the hordes of Russian Codiacks, the islanders were induced to abandon their homes and seek protection on the mainland.

(19) The Mission of San Gabriel that stands in the center of the grand valley of Santa Anita, and the most fertile portion of Los Angeles county.

(20) The reverend Friar, Junipero Serra, who headed a band of missionaries to this coast in the year 1769, when he commenced his grand work of subjecting and Christianizing the rude Indian race of California. He located his first Mission at this place, afterward increased by a chain of missionary posts, twenty in number, extending to the northern shores of San Pablo Bay, gathering around them a crude population of from fifteen to twenty thousand Indians, which, under the direction and guidance of their spiritual fathers, were taught the most useful requirements. Some were carpenters, some were blacksmiths, others saddlers and shoemakers, and herders of the vast numbers of cattle, which, in course of time, accumulated to hundreds of thousands. The female department was taught spinning and weaving, and all the necessary requirements of household economy, so that they lived along a life of contentment and ease, with rarely a case of insubordination.

(21) Don Juan Bandini, who came to this country from Lima, with his father, who was an Italian by birth, and who had commanded a Spanish ship-of-war in early days. Don Juan, from his urbanity and pleasing manners, was very popular, and had always taken an active part in the interests of California, having represented her in the halls of the Monte-

zumas. His descendants were numerous, and were celebrated everywhere for their beauty and attractive manners.

(22) Captain Henry D. Fitch and Joseph Snooks, both were captains of ships plying between this coast and Lima. The former was an American, who came here in early days, a native of New Hampshire, and the latter was a European, who had resided many years on the South American coast.